I dedicate this book to my four children,

Hope, Alex, Joseph, and Michael,

for always asking me to read "just one

more" before bed every night.

Thanks for your support.

Amy

an imprint of Amplify Publishing Group

www.mascotbooks.com

HANSEL GETS RESCUED

For more information, please contact
Mascot Books, an imprint of Amplify Publishing Group
620 Herndon Parkway #320
Herndon, VA 20170
info@mascotbooks.com

Library of Congress Control Number: 2021925117

CPSIA Code: PRT0322A
ISBN-13: 978-1-63755-288-9

Printed in the United States

Hansel Gets Rescued

Amy Baker

Illustrated by Chiara Civati

Hansel the cat was born in a big house in the big city of Houston, which is in one of the biggest states of all: **Texas.**

A little old lady lived in the big house along with a lot of cats. Hansel had many brother and sister cats, cousin cats, and aunt and uncle cats. There were way too many cats for one house and one little old lady.

It was hard for the little old lady to feed all the cats or play with them, so Hansel usually went hungry, and sometimes he was **sad** or **lonely** or **scared.**

Hansel usually had to leave the big house to find food.
Sometimes he would get into fights with other cats over food.

Sometimes he won and got to eat, but sometimes he lost and
then he had to go hungry.

One day, Hansel saw the old lady
making a phone call.
She sounded very sad.

The next morning, several strangers came to the big house. They **chased the cats** and caught them and put them in cages.

Hansel was scared and tried to hide under the porch.
Strangers had never been nice to Hansel before, so
he was afraid of people—except for the old lady.
He had never learned to trust anyone else.

Hansel was not able to get away.
He was finally caught and loaded in a
truck and hauled away with the rest of the cats.

When the truck finally came to a stop, he was unloaded at a place called a **shelter** and put into a bigger cage. There were lots of cats there. Some of them he knew. Some of them he didn't.

He was scared, but there was food and water there, which made him feel better.

Hansel ate all his food and fell asleep in the corner of his cage. **Being afraid can make you tired.** Hansel was very tired.

Someone opened the cage which woke Hansel. **He felt scared again.** The strangers put him in a tub of water and used soap to clean him. Hansel put up a fight. *Cats were supposed to clean themselves,* he thought.

Another person made him swallow some pills and gave him some shots. Hansel put up a fight again, but it only hurt a little.

Hansel wasn't happy, but when he was put back in his cage, there was more food and water for him.

He ate it all and fell back asleep. He was still scared,
but for the first time ever, he wasn't hungry.

Hansel stayed in his new cage for many days. He had to take more medicine and he didn't get to run around, but he always had food to eat.

He took lots of naps and gave himself a bath every day. He was getting bigger, and his orange hair was no longer dirty.

He didn't have to fight anymore and the people at the shelter were always nice.

One day, Hansel and the other cats from the big house were **loaded into another big truck.** Hansel was scared. He didn't know where they were going.

They rode for many hours before they stopped again.
He tried to sleep, but **he was nervous** about
where he was going and why it was taking so long.

When they stopped, he could tell that the air was cooler. Hansel and the other cats were in a new place called Colorado. Their cages were unloaded and they were taken into a new shelter. Hansel was still scared but happy to see there was food and water here, too.

Hansel needed a foster home quick. The next
day he was loaded into a small cage again. A
stranger named Amy came and picked him up
and **took him home.**

It was scary at first, but the home was clean and quiet. Amy lived alone and always talked in a soothing voice. There were toys for Hansel to play with and there was always plenty of food and water.

Even though Amy was a stranger, Hansel saw that
she was kind and would care for him.
Hansel had a new home and maybe even a new friend.

About the Author

Amy Baker worked as a pediatric speech pathologist for twenty years. A mother of four and a grandmother of one, she has had the pleasure of reading more children's books than she can count over the years. Now that her children are grown, she has been able to start a new chapter in life by fulfilling a lifelong dream of writing her own book. When the pandemic hit and forced everyone into lockdown, Amy looked for companionship in a foster cat and her first story was born. A small-town transplant from North Dakota, Amy relocated to Denver, Colorado, in 2018.